Golden
Oldies

Written by
Jenny Jinks

Illustrated by
Kelly Caswell

Chapter 1

"You can't be serious," Jem said, staring at the rundown building of Golden Gates. "We actually have to live here? I thought you were joking!"

When Mum had told Jem that they were moving to a new town to run a retirement home, Jem hadn't really minded. And when she had heard that Summerville was known as the luckiest town in the world, Jem was actually quite excited.

It was about time her luck changed.

But as they turned down the overgrown driveway of Golden Gates, Jem's hopes popped like a balloon. It seemed that even the luckiest town in the world couldn't change her luck.

"It just needs a little bit of love," said Mum. "When it's done you'll have plenty of room to run around with your friends."

What friends? thought Jem. When everyone heard that she lived with a load of grannies, nobody would want anything to do with her.

Chapter 2

As it was the school holidays, Mum expected Jem to spend all her time helping out. Jem didn't really like old people, or the 'Golden Oldies' as they called themselves at Golden Gates. All they did was nap, knit, and drink lots of tea. Jem couldn't think of anything worse.

Jem was desperate to meet someone her own age, but there was no chance of that when the

the only people she saw were closer in age to the dinosaurs than to her. That was until Jem spotted a girl on her bike talking to one of the residents, Mrs Fletcher. Mrs Fletcher passed the girl a package, and the girl cycled away.

That's a bit odd, Jem thought. She wondered who the girl might be, and hoped she would see her again.

Jem didn't have to wait long. The next day, as she was wheeling the tea trolley along the corridor, Jem almost bumped right into the girl.

"Oh, I'm sorry," Jem gasped. "Can I help you?"

"I'm visiting my grandma," the girl said.

"Mrs Fletcher?" Jem asked.

The girl nodded. "I'm Alexa."

Jem and Alexa chatted as they walked together. Jem wished she could stay and chat for longer—it felt so nice talking to someone her own age. But she had a long list of jobs to get done by the end of the day. So she dragged herself reluctantly away.

Chapter 3

A little while later, Jem was taking some boxes out to the recycling when she overheard Alexa and Mrs Fletcher by the front door.

"You have the address, just leave it outside like we said. They are in for such a surprise!"

Jem peered round the side of the hedge to see Mrs Fletcher handing Alexa another package. What were they up to?

Then Alexa turned towards her. Jem didn't want them to think she was spying! She rushed behind the bin, tripped and pulled the bin down on top of her.

"Oh!" said Alexa in surprise. "Are you okay?"

She helped Jem up.

"I'm fine," Jem said, brushing the rubbish off herself. "What have you got there?"

Alexa looked awkwardly at the package.

"It's nothing. Just some biscuits Grandma gave me to take home. I'd better go. Bye!"

Jem watched as Alexa jumped on her bike and quickly cycled away.

Why would Alexa lie to her about the package?

Jem had a funny feeling that something wasn't

quite right at Golden Gates.

Chapter 4

Jem began to notice more strange things too: whispered conversations that stopped the moment she walked in the room, strange notes written on crossword puzzles. And what was with all the tea? Nobody could really drink that much. Very suspicious.

And Alexa had been so friendly that first day but now Jem barely got more than a quick 'hello'.

Alexa came over most days. Sometimes she would sit with the Golden Oldies for ages, deep in conversation. Other times, she would only stay a few minutes before cycling off again, a package or envelope tucked into her backpack.

Jem decided it was time to investigate. And to do that, she was going to have to get to know the Golden Oldies a bit better. She was going to join... the knitting club.

Click-clack clickety-clack went the knitting needles.

Tick-tick-tick went the clock.

This is so dull, thought Jem.

"Hasn't the weather been lovely," said Mr Bold.

"Very nice for this time of year," Mrs Fletcher said.

Click-clack-click.

"Wasn't it lucky that little Sammy's bike was found," said Jean.

"I heard that this town is full of luck," Jem said.

"Oh yes, the luckiest," Mrs Fletcher said with a smile. The room fell silent again.

Click-click clack-clack.

This is hopeless, thought Jem.

She wasn't learning anything. And was it her imagination, or was the clicking starting to sound a lot like Morse code? These Golden Oldies were clearly too clever to give up their secrets. It was time Jem did some serious investigating.

Chapter 5

Every evening like clockwork, the Golden Oldies

went out for a walk around the block. As soon

as they left, Jem took her chance and snuck into

Mrs Fletcher's room to look for clues. Everything

seemed normal.

Then Jem heard a creak outside. She quickly

hid under the bed just as the door opened.

Jem held her breath as Mum came in and put

something on the side. As soon as Mum was gone, Jem wriggled back out and her foot hit something under the bed. It was a box full of papers. Jem had a quick flick through. There were lists of names and addresses here in Summerville, and even maps of the area. What did Mrs Fletcher need these for?

Jem wanted to take a closer look but she heard voices outside the window. The Golden Oldies were back!

Jem shoved the box back under the bed and dashed out just as the group came through the front door.

"Shall I fetch the tea?" Jem asked.

"No thank you, dear," said Jean. "After all that excitement, I think we need a lie down."

Jem's mind was reeling. What were the Golden Oldies doing with all that information about the town? And what could possibly be so exciting about a walk around the block?

Jem had a feeling that whatever was going on, they were all in on it together. Maybe they were spies? Or criminals? Jem wasn't sure. But the answer must be in that box. She had to get another look.

So the next day, while the residents were having morning tea, Jem snuck straight back into Mrs Fletcher's room, pretending to change the sheets. But the box was gone. How was she going to find out what they were up to when the one bit of evidence had completely disappeared?

Then Jem heard Alexa arrive on her bike. Alexa must know something. Jem just needed to get her on her own. When Alexa rushed through the door, Jem was there to greet her.

"Hi!" Jem said brightly. "Want to help me make the tea?"

"Sorry, Jem, I can't today," Alexa puffed, and she made a beeline for her grandma.

This is going to be tricky, Jem thought. There was only one thing to do. Jem got her bike and hid by the front hedge. Just as she expected, Alexa soon came out with a small package and cycled off. Jem followed her.

Chapter 6

Jem made sure to keep at a safe distance as she followed Alexa around Summerville. Finally, Alexa stopped and jumped off her bike. Jem tucked her bike behind a tree out of sight. She watched as Alexa got the package out of her bag and opened it. Alexa began to walk up the street, scattering something on the ground as she went.

What is she up to? Jem wondered, darting from tree to shrub, hiding behind cars and signposts as she followed Alexa. Finally, Alexa stopped outside a house and emptied the last few strands of what looked like weeds on the front step, and then hid round the side of the house.

Jem couldn't believe Alexa would do something so mean!

"What are you doing, dumping weeds outside some poor person's house?!" Jem demanded, jumping from her hiding place and storming over.

"Wait, you don't understand!" Alexa said, startled.

"I thought we could be friends," Jem said. "But I don't think I want to be friends with someone who plays mean tricks."

Jem started trying to clean up the weeds with her hands when a cat came over to her and rubbed itself against her.

"Shoo!" Jem said as another cat appeared, and another after that.

What on earth is going on? Jem wondered. And then she realised... it wasn't weeds, it was catnip! Cats loved it!

Just then the front door opened.

"What is all this shouting out here?" the lady asked. And then she gasped.

"I can explain..." Jem said. But the woman didn't look angry, she looked happy.

"Mr Fluffykins!" she cried, scooping a fluffy cat up into a big cuddle. "He's been missing for days. Where did you find him?"

Jem looked at Alexa, who put her finger to her lips.

"He must have found his way home," Jem said, quickly shoving the catnip into her pockets.

"This really is the luckiest town in the world," the lady said. And she carried Mr Fluffykins inside the house.

Suddenly Jem gasped.

"It's you!" she cried, pointing at Alexa. "You're behind the luck in the town!"

Chapter 7

"Keep your voice down," Alexa hissed. "Yes, we are. It was Grandma's idea. The Golden Oldies have been helping the town out for years. But it's a secret. You can't tell anyone."

"But why?" Jem asked. "Shouldn't everyone know who to thank?"

"It's not that simple. Promise not to say anything. If people know who is behind the nice deeds they will only start asking for things. This way it's just a nice surprise. A bit of a mystery," Alexa said.

"I'm sorry I thought you were up to no good," Jem said.

"That's okay," Alexa said. "I'm sorry I had to keep it secret from you. We should probably tell Grandma that you know."

Alexa and Jem cycled back to Golden Gates, where Alexa quickly explained to her grandmother what had happened.

"Well," Mrs Fletcher said, peering at Jem over the top of her glasses. "It seems we have a super sleuth among us, hmmm?"

Jem stared at her shoes, blushing.

"We could use Jem's expert sneaking skills on our team, Grandma," Alexa said.

Jem looked up in shock. "Really?" she squeaked.

Mrs Fletcher smiled. "I think you're right, Alexa. I'm sure you could use help with your deliveries and reporting back on town gossip. There's only so much we can learn on our evening walks."

"I knew you weren't just going for a stroll around the block!" Jem said. "And the crossword club? That's just a cover too. And the knitting in Morse code?"

"I don't know what you're talking about," Mrs Fletcher said with a twinkle in her eye that told Jem that she was right about all of it.

Chapter 8

Jem was so excited to be part of the Golden Oldies. But she was still so busy around Golden Gates that she didn't have much time to help with their missions.

"There you are!" said Alexa, finding Jem in the garden hacking through a forest of weeds. "Want to come and help me deliver a... *secret package?*" Alexa whispered the last bit.

"I'm sorry, I can't today," Jem sighed. "Mum wants this all sorted by the weekend." She pointed at the jungle that might once have been a garden.

"Oh, that can wait," said Mrs Fletcher, coming outside with a hamper. "Take this picnic, have some fun. What harm will a couple of hours do? I've checked with your mum. Now off you go!"

"Thanks!" Jem said, and they grabbed the picnic basket and hopped on their bikes.

Jem and Alexa delivered the package—a cake for Mr Lions's birthday—and hid behind a wall to watch. Jem felt a buzz of excitement seeing how happy he was, and knowing that she'd had a

little something to do with it. She felt a bit like a

superhero with a secret identity.

Jem and Alexa explored Summerville together, and ate the delicious picnic at the park. When they got back to Golden Gates, Jem felt happier than she had in a long time.

Then she remembered the garden. There was so much left to do.

"I'll help," Alexa offered kindly. And they went out the back.

They both stopped and stared. The garden looked beautiful. The lawn was mowed, the weeds had vanished and there were even pretty little flowers in the borders. Jem felt a pang of guilt. Mum must have had to work really hard to get this done.

"This looks amazing, Jem!" Mum said, coming into the garden with the Golden Oldies. "I can't believe you're done already!"

But if Mum didn't sort the garden, then who...

thought Jem.

Then she spotted Mrs Fletcher discreetly

brushing some soil from her blouse.

"I had a bit of help from some friends," Jem

said.

"Well, aren't you lucky," Mum said.

Jem looked up at the Golden Oldies, and then round at Alexa, and she grinned. Maybe the town's luck was rubbing off on her after all.

Discussion Points

1. Why was Jem not happy to move to Golden Gates at first?

2. Which club did Jem join to investigate the Golden Oldies?
a) The crossword club
b) The knitting club
c) The jigsaw club

3. What was your favourite part of the story?

4. Who put catnip outside someone's house?

5. Why else do you think the Golden Oldies wanted to keep their luck giving a secret?

6. Who was your favourite character and why?

7. There were moments in the story when Jem had to **investigate**. Where do you think the story shows this most?

8. What do you think happens after the end of the story?

Book Bands for Guided Reading

The Institute of Education book banding system is a scale of colours that reflects the various levels of reading difficulty. The bands are assigned by taking into account the content, the language style, the layout and phonics. Word, phrase and sentence level work is also taken into consideration.

The Maverick Readers Scheme is a bright, attractive range of books covering the pink to grey bands. All of these books have been book banded for guided reading to the industry standard and edited by a leading educational consultant.

To view the whole Maverick Readers scheme, visit our website at

www.maverickearlyreaders.com

Or scan the QR code to view our scheme instantly!

Maverick Chapter Readers

(From Lime to Grey Band)